It happened ...one day

Tales of wit, courage, decisiveness and virtue

AF578080

Sandeep Singh Rai

INDIA • SINGAPORE • MALAYSIA

Copyright © Sandeep Singh Rai 2023
All Rights Reserved.

ISBN 979-8-89233-337-5

This book has been published with all efforts taken to make the material error-free after the consent of the author. However, the author and the publisher do not assume and hereby disclaim any liability to any party for any loss, damage, or disruption caused by errors or omissions, whether such errors or omissions result from negligence, accident, or any other cause.

While every effort has been made to avoid any mistake or omission, this publication is being sold on the condition and understanding that neither the author nor the publishers or printers would be liable in any manner to any person by reason of any mistake or omission in this publication or for any action taken or omitted to be taken or advice rendered or accepted on the basis of this work. For any defect in printing or binding the publishers will be liable only to replace the defective copy by another copy of this work then available.

DEDICATION

I dedicate this book to my respected teacher, Mrs. Mary Philips, who encouraged and inspired me to read good books. She gave her precious time to read and correct my compositions in English language and gave invaluable suggestions which helped me to develop my style of writing. I shall always be grateful and indebted to her.

Author

CONTENTS

FOREWORD

I recall with profound joy, the time when Sandeep Singh Rai, the author of this book first published some of his stories in a children's magazine. My sons really enjoyed reading those stories written by him. Over the years he has published many stories and articles on science for the young readers. All of which have been well received.

This book is a motley collection of some of his new stories which reflect the many facets of our lives.

In some stories you will also enjoy reading about the animal characters who acted very boldly to set things right.

As a close friend, I wish the author the very best for the success of his first book.

I feel the title of the book 'It happened....one day' is very appropriate for the incidents described in the stories contained in this book.

I sincerely hope that he will produce many more wondrous stories for his readers in times to come.

I wish him all success for the future.

Dr Topi Basar

Head of Department of Law

Rajiv Gandhi University

Rono Hills, Doimukh

Arunachal Pradesh

India.

PREFACE

The stories contained in 'It happened ...one day' are works of fiction. The characters of these stories are imaginary. But some of the incidents described therein are based on true happenings.

The human protagonists in these stories handle the situations they come face to face with, in a positive and receptive manner. In all the stories their presence of mind, wit, intelligence and strength of character shine through in many ways.

The animal characters are forced to make some tough choices in order to ensure their survival and to keep things moving in a positive direction. They rise to the occasion and exhibit fine qualities of daring, good planning, camaraderie and sheer courage.

These stories do convey subtle messages which can be delicately perceived.

All in all, these stories portray positive action, good thinking, keen perception and smart execution on the part of the characters.

I sincerely hope that the readers will read and reflect upon them in a myriad ways.

Author

ACKNOWLEDGEMENT

I would like to thank my daughter, Amrita, who has always loved to hear my stories. It was her unique ideas which brought these stories to life in the present form.

I am highly grateful to my wife, Dr. Awekta, for her careful and critical reading of the manuscript. She also pointed out the shortcomings therein and gave valuable suggestions for its improvement. She was also a big help in the editing of these stories, without which these stories would never have seen the light of the day.

All the errors and omissions in the stories which may be apparent to the readers are my mistakes and suggestions for improvement are welcome.

Author

THE RESCUE

Ravi and Nitin were two fishermen who lived in a small coastal village in southern India. They were very good friends. Together they would go fishing and when the day's catch was sold they shared the money equally amongst themselves.

One day, as they were fishing in the deep sea they felt a sudden turbulence under their boat. The next moment their boat was sucked into the water.

The fishermen, to their utter amazement, realized that they could breathe underwater! It was very dark undersea but the visibility was quite good as the water was clear. They could see the sea bed. They saw the marine plants swaying in the current of the sea and various kinds of fishes that went past them.

Suddenly their vicinity was lit up! They were surrounded by sharks, dressed as soldiers. They held spears pointing at Ravi and Nitin.

The two friends got very scared as the sharks looked menacing. The feeling of relief at not having drowned in the deep sea simply vanished. They noticed that the 'shark-soldiers' were saying something which was unintelligible to them and making angry gestures. They inferred that they were asking them to march ahead of them in a particular direction. They had no choice but to obey them.

They were made to march to a palace made of icicles whose gates were guarded by even more menacing 'shark-soldiers' numbering at least a dozen. These guards, on seeing the soldiers approaching the palace with two prisoners opened the gates for them.

Inside, was a long passage down which the two fishermen were urged to proceed. The passage widened into a large hall which was lined with large columns of coral. At each column a shark-soldier stood guard. The place was crowded with sea creatures of many kinds.

Moving on, a little farther, the two friends saw a large dolphin sitting on a throne made of huge seashells. Ravi and Nitin were very nervous and they looked around anxiously.

"She must be the queen of this underwater empire" thought the two of them.

The soldiers leading the two fishermen bowed courteously before her and this confirmed their guess.

On seeing Ravi and Nitin brought before her in this manner, she asked one of the soldiers who had captured Ravi and Nitin, "Why have you brought them here?"

The soldier answered, "Your Majesty! These two fishermen were fishing in our territory, that's why we have captured them and brought them here."

Looking around, Ravi and Nitin could see all eyes now turned towards them and they understood that all the sea creatures present were the courtiers and the subjects of the queen.

They realized with an uneasy feeling that they had been ushered in at a time when the queen was holding court and some important matters were being discussed. The queen was very annoyed at being interrupted in the middle of a meeting where important matters were being brought to her knowledge.

Ravi, gathering a little courage said, "Your Majesty! Why have they captured us? It is not an offence to fish in the deep sea!"

The queen looked at him and said in a sad voice, "A few days ago, some fishermen were fishing in the nearby territory and they caught my daughter, the 'Dolphin-princess' in their net and took her away. I sent my soldiers to look for her but all our efforts to find her failed." Saying so, the queen burst into tears.

The fishermen pitied her. Ravi suddenly recalled something!

He said to the queen, "Your Majesty! A fisherman named Rajan, who lives in our neighbouring village catches and sells exotic sea creatures. He usually sells them to the rich and fashionable customers of nearby cities. If we approach him, maybe, we can find something about the whereabouts of the dolphin-princess. If you permit us, we can try and get a lead for your search for the dolphin-princess from him."

On hearing this, the queen's eyes lit up with hope and she asked longingly, "Can you bring my daughter back?"

Nitin bowed before her and replied courteously, "Your Majesty, we shall do our best to bring her back."

"Tell me if you need help with something" the Queen said.

Ravi replied, "We will need some fine clothes."

"OK! You shall be given fine clothes and my minister will go with you to help you recognize the princess and see that you don't escape" said the Queen. She ordered one of her attendants to give them fine clothes.

She summoned her prime minister who was also a shark and he was to accompany the two fishermen to Rajan's village. The two friends put on the clothes brought for them and accompanied by the minister, who had now transformed into a man, went ashore in their boat which had arisen to the surface from the deep sea by some unknown force.

Ravi and Nitin rowed their boat to a quiet part of the shore and moored it to a coconut tree. All of them disembarked quietly and they proceeded on foot down a narrow dirt track leading to Rajan's village.

On reaching the village, they made some inquiries and located Rajan's house. They checked their appearance before approaching his house.

After having made sure that everything was in order, they entered Rajan's house. The house was surrounded by an enclosure made of woven mats of coconut leaves. The courtyard was full of large jars which on closer inspection they found, contained many types of sea creatures inside them. They looked for Rajan as they moved across the courtyard and found him sitting on a cot in a corner of the courtyard behind some empty jars.

They went up to him. He was a little surprised to see the three finely dressed gentlemen.

Ravi introduced themselves by saying, "We have come from the neighbouring kingdom" and pointing at the queen's minister in the guise of a man, stated respectfully, "And he is the prime minister of Her Majesty, The Queen."

The minister taking the cue from this formal introduction said "We want to purchase an exquisite present for the Queen, as it is her birthday day after tomorrow."

Rajan was very pleased to hear that, he eagerly awaited such distinguished and wealthy customers. He sensed an excellent opportunity of making good money. Getting up from his cot hurriedly, he excitedly led them into a large room, where he showed them many sea creatures like crabs, tortoises, jelly fishes, squids and sting rays etc.

The visitors just shook their heads to show their lack of interest in the common stuff.

He sensed their apparent lack of interest. Being driven by a keen desire to make a handsome profit from these customers, he did not want to let go of a rare and golden opportunity such as this one.

Rajan thought for a moment and said to them, "I want to show you a rare and unique specimen!"

"Please follow me" he said and he asked them to follow him deeper inside his house.

He went ahead and opened a trapdoor and began to climb down some steps to a cellar and gestured to the three men to follow him. He cautioned his customers, "Be careful, while walking down the steps and please mind the low ceiling!"

Next, he led them all to a huge jar kept on a sideboard. Taking off the cloth covering the jar, he exclaimed, "This is the best one I have and it is very expensive!"

It was a very beautiful young dolphin! Ravi and Nitin were taken aback by the spectacle! They had never seen anything like it before. The minister gently nudged Ravi to signal that it was indeed the missing dolphin-princess.

"Oh! Never mind, we can pay you in gold coins, just tell us the price" said the minister in a very generous manner.

Rajan cleared his throat and quoted greedily, "500 gold coins."

"That's too much!" exclaimed Nitin.

Rajan thought for a moment and said, "I will give it to you for 450 gold coins, not less than that."

"OK!" said the minister and shook hands with Rajan and assured him that they would be back in the evening with the required gold coins as payment and also instructed him that he should keep the dolphin properly packed, ready for shipment to their kingdom.

The minister then taking Ravi and Nitin along ventured towards the marketplace.

"My dear friends, I have a plan that will help us to get the princess away from here and at the same time teach this greedy man a lesson" he said when they were away from the crowd in the market. He hurriedly whispered something into the fishermen's ears and they nodded in agreement.

It was almost evening when they returned to Rajan's house after having visited the nearby town.

He was eagerly waiting for them. The minister handed him a small sack and said, "Here are your 450 gold coins."

Rajan grabbed the sack filled with gold coins and opened it then and there. His eyes shone with amazement on seeing its contents.

"Yes, yes! Thank you! And here's the lovely creature you have selected as a gift for your queen, all ready for shipment" he said pointing to the large jar that contained the dolphin-princess.

The minister clapped his hands in glee and Nitin on cue, brought forth a bottle of fine foreign wine and asked Rajan to fetch four glasses to pour the drink for all of them.

"Let's drink to the happiness and long life of the Queen! Nitin said, as he handed the bottle of wine to Rajan.

They were now to execute the most sensitive and important part of their plan. Rajan brought the four glasses and hurriedly poured forth the wine for all of them. He gulped down his glassful in no time, without even waiting for the others. They could just look at him in surprise when he quickly poured himself another glassful and drank it too.

Shortly thereafter, he began to sway on his feet and slumped to the floor. Soon he fell asleep.

The wine laced with sleeping pills had done the job!

Nitin and Ravi carried him to a nearby cot and put him down.

The minister cast a quick look about the place and picked up the sack of coins. On seeing that nobody was around and thus grabbing the opportunity, the fishermen with the minister's help quickly carried the jar containing the dolphin- princess. It had been covered properly with tarpaulin. They hurriedly moved away towards their boat.

Nobody seemed to notice anything as it was dusk and the village folk were busy in their homes with their evening chores.

On reaching the boat, Ravi and Nitin hastily emptied the jar into a large tub fitted into their boat. The dolphin-princess on being released from her captivity smiled at them and murmured some words of gratefulness.

They rowed their boat swiftly and went far away into the sea.

Suddenly, the minister snapped his fingers and he transformed into a shark again and the boat was sucked into the sea. They sank to the seabed and immediately made their way to the palace of the Queen along with the dolphin-princess. The Queen was overjoyed to see her daughter and she embraced the princess tightly and kissed her forehead.

She rewarded the two fishermen for their good deed by giving them a lot of gems and jewels and other valuable items. They were also given the bagful of gold coins as a special reward!

She thanked Ravi and Nitin profusely and then asked her guards to respectfully escort them back to their boat.

As they were seated in their boat, it rose to the surface of the sea and they were able to row it towards the shore.

On reaching the shore, they headed home.

When they were safely home, they divided their treasure equally and showed it to their families. They had become rich.

On coming to know of their good fortune, their neighbours curiously asked them, "Where did you get so much of the riches?"

The friends merrily replied, "We caught a treasure-chest full of gems and jewels!"

They had been amply rewarded for their good deed. And they lived happily ever after.

DOCTOR! BE CAREFUL

Doctors and physicians are the healers of the society. They are expected to practise their profession with due diligence and care. This means that they have to be very careful while treating their patients.

Sometimes, however, they forget to ensure their own safety and well-being. Dr. Dutta realized this important fact, the hard way; through the mischief of a little boy who accompanied his mother to his clinic.

Dr. Dutta was a general physician who practised his profession in a good locality of Delhi. He enjoyed a good reputation and over the years he had built a very good practice. He had a large number of patients who came to his clinic for various ailments.

Dr. Dutta had graduated from the prestigious Maulana Azad Medical College in Delhi and had earned his MBBS degree. He had developed very good clinical skills and provided relief and succour to countless patients of the locality. So much so that his fame had slowly spread to nearby areas.

Sometimes a patient would turn up at his clinic and say, "Doctor Sahib! My relative was cured by you and he talks very highly of you." Dr. Dutta very humbly acknowledged the praise showered upon him by his patients.

Modesty and honesty were Dr. Dutta's great virtues apart from his immaculate clinical skills.

His clinic was situated on the main road of the locality. He had preferred it to be located on the ground floor for easy access to all patients. It was a spacious clinic which was very hygienically maintained. It consisted of the waiting room for the patients, the consultation room where the doctor examined his patients, a small operatory where minor surgical procedures could be done and adjoining it was the pharmacy for dispensing medicines.

Sister Disha was the nurse and helper who assisted Dr. Dutta in his work every morning and evening. She had a very pleasing personality and was very friendly and mild mannered. Her words of kindness put the patients at ease and were a useful recipe for curing the patients. So, she had an important role to play in the success and good reputation of Dr. Dutta's clinic.

Mr. Ashutosh, the pharmacist was responsible for dispensing the medicines to the patients and for instructing them in taking the medicines in a proper and desirable manner. He was very polite and soft spoken.

He often advised the patients by saying, "In order to get well and for the success of your treatment, please take your medicines properly as advised. In case of any doubt, you can ask me any time."

The patients listened to him carefully and followed his instructions down to the last detail. Mr. Ashutosh was always very frank with the patients and clearly told them about the medicines not available at his pharmacy.

"These medicines are not available at our pharmacy. Hence you have to buy them from the chemist. Please make sure that you understand the proper dosage" he advised them.

Thus, Dr. Dutta with the help of his dedicated and efficient staff continued to practise his profession and brought smiles to innumerable patients who visited him.

One day, late in the evening, a lady came to his clinic accompanied by her son. She had severe pain in the abdomen and had vomited several times during the day. Her five years old son had accompanied her out of curiosity.

The husband of the lady was away for some office work and was to come home late in the evening. He had advised her to go to Dr. Dutta on her own and take their son, Raman, along. Raman could not have been left at home alone in any case.

So, Mrs. Shanti went to Dr. Dutta's clinic late in the evening. There were just two patients waiting to see him, before her.

Sister Disha walked up to her when she was seated in the waiting room and said, "The doctor will see you soon. Is there anything I can do to help you?"

Mrs. Shanti smiled despite her discomfort and replied thankfully, "No Sister, I will wait for my turn."

Sister Disha reassured her, "The doctor has been very busy this evening but he will definitely help you."

Sister Disha was soon called away by Dr. Dutta to help him change the dressings on the wound of an elderly man.

The patients before Shanti were attended to in due course of time. They collected their medicines from Mr. Ashutosh and went away. All this time, Raman sat beside his mother and carefully observed the people and the place.

Mrs. Shanti was called by the doctor for consultation. She walked slowly to the consultation room with Raman holding onto her hand and walking shyly beside her.

Dr. Dutta examined her carefully and listened to her complaint. While the doctor was busy with examining Mrs. Shanti, 'the little imp'- Raman had not been idle. He had quickly taken in his surroundings and had carefully observed everything in the doctor's consultation room.

In what was to be Dr. Dutta's misfortune and an embarrassing situation for him, Raman sighted an empty syringe with needle lying on the doctor's table.

What more does a naughty boy need! He picked it up out of curiosity and as Dr. Dutta was examining his mother and had his back to him, Raman silently approached him from behind and jabbed the needle of the syringe in his back side and left it there.

Dr. Dutta howled loudly with pain. "O my God! What's this? he shouted. Then looking at his side, he saw the syringe embedded in his back side and Raman standing next to him, frozen with fear.

Dr. Dutta quickly pulled the syringe out of his back side and after hastily destroying the needle he disposed it of in the waste bin. He had felt the pain of the unwanted injection given to him by the small boy. But more than that, he was dismayed at his own carelessness.

The needle and syringe had been used by him on an earlier patient and he had negligently left it lying on the table. He had forgotten to dispose it of due to the rush of the patients that evening. It was an open invitation for the mischievous little boy.

Dr. Dutta quickly realized his mistake and understood the scenario created by his carelessness. He was visibly shaken and tried to calm himself down with the words, "I have been very careless today and my mistake could even have resulted in injury to the boy."

Mrs. Shanti stood there shocked at Raman's action and started scolding him. Raman started crying.

Sister Disha and Ashutosh rushed to the doctor's room on hearing his cry of pain and the following commotion. Sister Disha got there first and she stood there looking from Raman to the doctor, not comprehending the cause of the ruckus.

She helped Dr. Dutta to his seat and asked softly, "What happened, doctor?"

Dr. Dutta described the incident in detail.

On hearing the doctor's version, she said apologetically, "Doctor! I understand what happened and it's my fault. I should have disposed of the syringe and needle immediately. The little boy is not to blame."

Mr. Ashutosh had halted at the entrance to the consultation room. He craned his neck to look inside. He suppressed his smile with a great effort after having come to know what had happened. He just pretended to merely look on but he could not stop himself from saying "First things, first!"

Dr. Dutta had recovered himself and he spoke slowly, saying, "We have been very busy this evening and this incident has brought home to us the message that all due care and diligence must be exercised at all times. Raman through his mischief has pointed out to us our grave omission."

"Mrs. Shanti, please don't feel bad and don't scold him. He has taught us a very important thing which we had neglected to follow due to our busy schedule" said the doctor humbly. He thanked Mrs. Shanti profusely.

She was discharged shortly thereafter, having been given clear instructions by Mr. Ashutosh to take her medicines and was asked to report back after three days.

After she had left, Dr. Dutta turned very seriously to his staff and said, "Today we have learnt a very important aspect of the practice of medical profession; that is, that we must be meticulous in the discharge of our duties in order to ensure our own safety and well-being and of those who seek our services."

"There's no room for *Negligence*" he added.

Mrs. Shanti went home with Raman and felt relieved to see that her husband had arrived back home. She narrated the events of the evening to him in great detail.

Her husband listened very carefully and couldn't stop laughing at the whole incident.

He was amused by the entire happenings but at the same time he was amazed at the doctor's receptive and positive attitude.

"Some people are pillars of the society" he remarked at length.

Raman was able to go scot free. He went to his room and started playing with his toy 'doctor's set'. He pulled out the plastic syringe from the box and looked at it wonderingly and thought, "What harm can this little thing possibly do to a doctor? I was just playing with it."

Who better than Dr. Dutta to answer his simple and innocent question!

CALL OF THE FOREST

A new day had dawned over the Green Forest and the trees shone in the early morning rays of the sun. A light mist hovered above the upper canopy of the trees. The denizens of the forest stirred slowly from their sleep and stretched themselves in preparation for an important day. This day was unlike other days, for they could feel urgency in the air!

'Haathiraj'–the elephant trudged to the central arena of the Green Forest accompanied by all the other senior animals. All residents of the forest knew from past experience that such a procedure was followed only when an important meeting of the Residents' Council was convened to discuss matters of prime concern to all of them. They had prior notice of the meeting but the agenda of the meeting was not disclosed in advance.

On reaching the central arena, all the senior animals including 'Haathiraj', 'Sher Singh'- the tiger, 'Greyhair'- the wolf, 'Dum-Dum'–the rhino, 'Jumpy'- the monkey and 'Massive'- the buffalo took their seats on the stumps of the trees that had been felled by the lumber contractor's men long ago. The proposed reforestation of the forest had not been carried out, much to the chagrin of the inhabitants.

The stumps of trees stood as grim epitaphs to the apathy of the authorities towards the preservation of the Green Forest.

On this day, as the animals started gathering in the arena in large numbers, they could notice the look of concern on the faces of all the seniors seated there. Some of the old residents of the forest among them, recalled the glorious past of the Green Forest when it was part of the princely state of Chanderpur in Central India.

It had been the royal hunting ground of the rulers of Chanderpur and was well preserved. Common people had not been allowed in the forest which was maintained in a pristine condition.

None could cut trees or cause any damage to the forest. There was severe punishment and penalty for disobeying the law in this regard.

Hunting or 'shikar' had been the prerogative of the royal family and their guests. The number of animals hunted in a season was carefully controlled so that no species of animals was over-exploited.

When the country attained independence from the colonial rulers, Chanderpur had merged with the rest of the country and kingship was abolished. The Green Forest had thus survived hunting of animals and cutting of trees; legal or illegal, up to that point of time.

However, in the present administrative set up of the country, the politicians had become the de-facto rulers.

The implementation of laws was lax due to various reasons. Lack of respect for the laws, corrupt officials and paucity of resources were just a few of them.

Things had slowly soured for the inhabitants of the Green Forest and their habitat; their homeland began to deteriorate right before their eyes. The golden dream of independence had been reduced to just that: **a Dream**!

They were jerked back to the Present, their reverie shattered, as Haathiraj said in a deep and booming voice, trying to capture their attention, "Friends and fellow-residents of the Green Forest!"

"Today we have gathered here to discuss a very grave matter which concerns us all and threatens our very existence and that of our home– Our Green Forest" he stated earnestly.

All the animals present there exchanged nervous glances on hearing these words. They could hardly imagine such a calamity befalling the Green Forest. They sat upright and listened attentively as Haathiraj motioned for Sher Singh to speak.

Sher Singh cleared his throat, adjusted his spectacles and held up the day's edition of the 'Forest Times'. He began to read the bold headlines and said "My dear fellow- inhabitants of the Green Forest! I must inform you that the government has decided to build a State Highway through our forest and what's even worse is, that for this undertaking at least 10,000 trees will have to be cut within a span of one year."

"This decision is in clear violation of the law and we shall oppose it with all our might, but in a non- violent manner" he stated emphatically.

All the animals present there were thunderstruck! Sher Singh rubbed his chin with his forepaw and carefully continued, "We are well aware of how in the past our forest has been depredated in the name of 'Development' and we have been pushed to the margins of what used to be our pristine Green Forest."

He could say no more and with moist eyes and a heavy heart he merely gestured towards the graveyard of trees around them. Everyone present understood what he meant by that gesture.

Sher Singh recovered himself and speaking passionately he stated, "Our elected representative, Lal Chand did not bother to consult us in this matter and he has not raised his voice against the proposed encroachment of our homeland and violation of our rights. Although he is our representative in the State Legislature, he has just been a mute observer as this decision was being taken to our disadvantage. Haathiraj and I had been to the city to see him in this regard when initial rumours of such a decision by the government started circulating. On raising this issue with him, we felt that he was not very open about discussing it with us and his reply to our direct inquiry had at best been evasive."

He stopped speaking and pointed towards all the gathered inhabitants. "We all must find some way to protect our forest in order to save our lives and to preserve it for our generations to come" he shouted.

"This is our Fundamental Right to Life and we shall fight to uphold it" he stated firmly.

These words of truth and wisdom, so passionately spoken, had their desired impact on the animals and they cheered loudly.

Suddenly 'Brownie'- the fox jumped up and asked nervously "What are we to do then? Is there a way to save our forest from this planned and illegal destruction?"

All animals had a grave look on their faces as they looked at the seniors for an answer.

Dum- Dum who had been quietly listening, now said, Yes! There is. But one that is long and hard. It shall need very careful planning and will test our unity and persistence" he cautioned.

"We all love our Green Forest and are willing to make all efforts to save it" said Brownie determinedly after having listened to what Dum-Dum had to say.

Meanwhile, Haathiraj had been in deep thought but now he stood up from his seat and began to explain what he considered to be the best plan to save Green Forest.

He spoke firmly and said, "We should plan to elect our representative to the State Assembly from among us in the forthcoming elections."

"He shall be the one to safeguard our rights more effectively and will be answerable to us, unlike Lal Chand who is loyal to his party and himself. The best way to fight for change in a system is to be a part of the system" he said encouragingly.

"In order to achieve this, we must first meet the Governor of the State and present a memorandum to him signed by all of us, demanding that the Green Forest electoral constituency be 'Reserved' for our candidate so that only a resident of the Green Forest can be elected to the State Assembly from this constituency. This will ensure a better safeguard of our rights and we will be able to voice our needs and concerns through a proper forum in future. We will also ask him to put a halt to the plan to construct the highway through our homeland" explained Haathiraj very patiently.

"But who all do you have in mind to contest these elections!" asked 'Whitetail'- the rabbit on hearing what Haathiraj had explained. It appealed to him as a great idea but such a big task was simply mind-boggling for the little fellow.

"How will we ensure that he represents us honestly and safeguards our interests" asked Massive.

"Can we nominate someone from among us unanimously as our candidate so that he can be elected unopposed as an 'Independent candidate'?" asked Brownie.

Everyone listened carefully to her, as all animals held Brownie in high esteem for her wisdom. It was well known that she had been one of the advisors to the erstwhile king of the Green Forest who was a vassal of the ruler of Chanderpur. Her advice and suggestions were eagerly sought and dutifully implemented.

Now that the animals had warmed up to the ideas being put forth in the meeting, they participated eagerly in the discussion. Haathiraj and all the other seniors were very pleased at the progress of the proceedings.

After having heard these new suggestions, being voiced by the residents, Haathiraj was satisfied that his message had sunk home. All animals, big and small who were present had now expressed their willingness and keen desire to plan for their future and to protect the Green Forest.

He spoke excitedly, "Friends! I am very happy that you have realized the importance of all that we are discussing here today and I think we can now plan a little further in order to form a consensus as to how and whom we want to nominate as our candidate for the elections. Out of all the proposed names, as Brownie rightly suggested, we shall propose the name of one candidate from among us to contest these elections as our 'Independent' candidate. I request that all of you please suggest one name each from among us for candidature."

"Just a small announcement before we disperse, please sign the memorandum which we shall hand over to the

Governor day after tomorrow when Haathiraj, Sher Singh and myself go to the city. There shall be another meeting in a week's time when we shall finalize the name of our candidate for the elections" said Dum-Dum trying to make himself heard above the whispering and murmuring that was now going on openly among the animals gathered there.

"We shall! We shall!" shouted all the animals in a loud chorus and slowly the meeting broke up with the animals moving away in small groups, talking excitedly among themselves.

They were very receptive to the idea of taking charge of their future and were anxiously looking forward to the next meeting.

Meanwhile, Lal Chand had received news of the dis-contentment among the residents of his constituency and the meeting held in the Green Forest. He quickly got busy in devising ways to save face and to safeguard his position in his political party at the same time.

The State funding for the proposed highway was giving him headaches as there was a scarcity of funds for the undertaking. There was much objection to this project from the opposition parties and the environmental activists were threatening to move the High Court against this project.

With the elections just round the corner, he had much to think and plan for because he wanted to retain his seat in the State Assembly and all the accompanying benefits and comforts too. The future of the forest and welfare of the animals were farthest to his mind.

The inhabitants of the Green Forest started working diligently to complete the list of all the probable candidates from among themselves.

The first names on the list were Haathiraj, Sher Singh, Dum-Dum and Brownie but some considered 'Greyhair'- the wolf and 'Spotty'- the chital deer to be deserving candidates.

In order to drum up support and enthusiasm for the proposed tasks, the following Notice had been put up at various places in the Green Forest for all to see:

ATTENTION: RESIDENTS OF GREEN FOREST.

We have all agreed to bring a 'Change' and in order to succeed, we must accomplish the following:

1. To put a halt to the construction of the State Highway through the heart of Green Forest.
2. To submit a memorandum to the Governor to this effect and at the same time to request him to 'Reserve' our constituency for our candidate in the forthcoming elections.
3. To prepare a list of all probable candidates from among us, one of whom can be nominated as our candidate.
4. To be ready for the next meeting in a week's time.

Lots more to do! See you soon!

Residents' Council of Green Forest

Haathiraj, Sher Singh and Dum-Dum went to the city to meet the Governor as planned. They put before him the signed memorandum and stressed the need to put on hold all plans of building the proposed highway.

Haathiraj also brought up their demand for a change in the method of representation of the residents of the forest in the State Assembly. He pointed out the apathy of the present government towards the residents of Green Forest and the callous attitude of Lal Chand.

The Governor was surprised and impressed at the same time by the unprecedented manner in which the animals had approached him to highlight their problems and concerns. He listened patiently and admired them for their sincerity and direct approach.

After hearing them, he explained to the delegates, the law in this regard, even as he expressed his inability to help them.

"The Governor cannot help you to reserve your constituency for your candidate as it is a legislative matter" he stated in plain words.

He further stated, "A bill to this effect shall have to be presented in the Parliament and passed by majority of votes. It shall then be made into a law and notified officially. The Election Commission also has a role to play in this matter."

He paused and then continued slowly, "Only then can it be implemented. As there is no session of the Parliament before the elections and with the elections fast approaching, this is no time for drastic changes and controversies. All political parties would want to steer clear of such a scenario."

"As for the construction of the highway, you shall read about it in the news shortly" said the Governor in a low voice, bending closer to the delegates. He winked at them after having said so.

The Governor's plain words and his inability to help them did not dampen the spirits of the three delegates and instead they asked, "We agree to what you say Sir, but what are we to do then?"

The Governor replied in a hushed voice, "You can field a 'consensus' Independent candidate of your choice and cast all your votes in his favour to elect him."

"OOOOOO!" said all three of them and having understood the true import of these words they sat back in a relaxed manner.

They thanked him profusely and took leave of him. They were very satisfied about the outcome of this meeting and were back in the Green Forest by evening.

The residents of Green Forest in the meantime had contacted the animals of the adjoining smaller forests and natural habitats which formed part of the electoral constituency of Green Forest. They had won them over to their common cause. All of them now stood strong and united and adequately prepared to take up the tasks ahead.

Just a day before the next meeting, the news headlines in the 'Forest Times' stated that the proposed plan to construct the highway through the forest had been put on hold. The environmental activists had filed a writ petition in the High Court and the court had granted an injunction in the matter. It had ordered the State to conduct a thorough assessment of the proposed undertaking and submit the Environmental Impact Assessment Report of the project as provided for under the Environment Protection Act.

This news which signified a small victory and some measure of relief brought a wave of happiness and cheer in the Green Forest. All of them heaved a sigh of relief!

The meeting was held the next day as planned and the residents of the surrounding areas which were part of the constituency of Green Forest also attended in large numbers. The meeting was presided over by Haathiraj who was considered the most experienced of them all. All other seniors were also present. They briefed the gathering about the discussion with the Governor and carefully outlined the task ahead in the light of the present scenario.

Haathiraj addressed them and said, "Friends! We have all heard the news that the plan to build the highway through our forest has been stayed but we must proceed as planned and in order to reap the full benefits of our ongoing movement; *we must strike the iron when it is hot!*"

"Thus, there will be no changes to our plans and we proceed as agreed" he added vehemently.

Sher Singh who spoke next, said, "We must prepare for the forthcoming elections and I shall read out the names of all the probable candidates that were submitted by you all."

He announced, "The names are Haathiraj, Dum-Dum, Brownie, Greyhair, Sher Singh, Jumpy, Spotty and Whitetail. In order to nominate just one name out of these, I shall look to the name that has been proposed by the maximum number of residents, and that is our friend 'Spotty'!"

"I therefore have no hesitation in nominating him as our 'Independent' candidate for the upcoming elections. Please give him a big applause" said Sher Singh excitedly as he himself clapped his hands in sheer joy.

There was a big round of applause and 'Spotty'- the deer stepped forward. He bowed to the gathering and acknowledged their greetings.

He thanked them all with these words, "Friends, I am well aware of the tough task ahead and the responsibility you all have given to me. I shall do my best to uphold your trust and fulfill your expectations. I thank all of you from the bottom of my heart and at the same time request you to be with me in the fight to save our Green Forest."

Some animals stepped forward and greeted him with bouquets of fresh flowers and flower petals were showered over him. There were loud cheers of 'Long live Spotty!' and 'Victory to Spotty!' All this was very pleasing to Spotty but at the same time he was well aware of the tough battle and the hard work that lay ahead.

All the political parties had fielded strong candidates for the constituency of Green Forest. The candidates who were contesting the elections including Spotty filed their nomination papers.

Green Forest was now very much in the news and had become a very hotly contested seat for the State Assembly.

The date of polling had been announced and the election propaganda began.

Spotty got very busy touring the entire constituency with his supporters and met almost all residents of Green Forest and the adjoining forests.

The candidates of other parties also visited Green Forest and held small meetings. They were generally accompanied by their supporters from their own respective parties. These meetings were not well-attended by the animals of the forest and all these other candidates found no support from the residents of the forest.

The residents of the forest chose to keep their 'Secret' close to their chest and to reveal it only much later at the polls.

Spotty's speeches at his meetings were brief and to the point. He promised to work for his fellow residents of Green Forest and to save the forest from the greedy politicians. He also promised not to let the road through the forest to be built at any cost.

Lal Chand was also in the fray as the candidate of his party. He made several visits to Green Forest and held many meetings hoping to salvage some credibility and gain support from the animals.

The animals had by now made up their minds for the polling day and they paid no heed to him. He was merely tolerated by them as an unavoidable and uninvited visitor.

The polling day was fast approaching and Spotty was very busy. Day by day his confidence had increased and he was sure that he had the complete and unconditional support of all inhabitants.

All eligible voters of Green Forest were anxiously waiting for the day of polling in order to show their unity and strength at the ballot.

There were to be five polling stations in the Green Forest to facilitate access for all voters.

Two days before the polling, the election propaganda ended, giving time to the voters to make up their minds. But in this case, their minds were already made up!

On the day of polling, all animals determinedly made their way to the polling stations to cast their votes. The

EVMs were introduced with a view to make voting very fast and precise. A very heavy rush was seen at all the polling stations right from early morning onwards.

Massive and Dum-Dum had organized the young residents into small groups and they had been stationed near all the polling stations. This was done to thwart any attempt by the hired goons of the political parties to interfere with the polling process or to intimidate the voters. In the evening the voting ended peacefully.

All eligible voters of Green Forest had cast their votes. The results were to be declared in two days.

The results of the elections were declared as scheduled and to everyone's joy and jubilation Spotty had been elected with a huge margin. The outcome of the elections was cheered by all residents of the forest.

There was celebration and merriment in the Green Forest as Spotty was carried in a procession to the beating of drums and cymbals and blowing of bugles. He organized a 'Thanksgiving ceremony' where Haathiraj, Sher Singh and Dum-Dum were the guests of honour.

He took the opportunity to thank everyone and said gracefully, "Friends! We have won a historic victory and I thank you all for this achievement. I have been entrusted with a big responsibility which I shall be able to discharge only with your support and help."

"This is a memorable moment in the history of Green Forest for now we shall have a say in the matters that concern us" he said and waved triumphantly to all his fellow- residents.

The residents of the Green Forest had indeed left everyone in the political circles astonished and the political bigwigs were mesmerized by their display of determination, solidarity and meticulous planning.

Spotty was the only 'Independent' candidate elected to the newly formed State Assembly. The previous ruling party had lost touch with the masses and was routed at the polls. It failed to win a majority.

A new coalition government was formed with a capable young man as the chief minister. He outlined the urgent tasks carefully and was open to the views of the opposition parties.

He admired Spotty for his courage and honesty. On Spotty's suggestion and on approval by a majority in the Assembly, a committee was constituted to promote eco-tourism in the Green Forest.

This was to be done in a way so as to benefit the animals and not to disturb the ecological balance in any way.

The plan to build the road through the forest was permanently dropped.

Spotty was greatly relieved on hearing this. He happily conveyed it to his friends in the Green Forest. He had fulfilled his promise to the residents of the Green Forest.

All the inhabitants of the Green Forest were ecstatic with joy and they cheered him excitedly when this news reached them.

With time and experience Spotty became a very capable and popular legislator. In the years to come, he won several terms to the State Assembly as the representative of Green Forest and served its residents conscientiously.

With their unity, determination and hard work the residents of Green Forest had saved their homeland from destruction. They had also conclusively proved to everyone, for all times to come, that preserving forests and environment is a beneficial venture and is also economically viable.

Their message was loud and clear, 'SAVE ENVIRONMENT AND FORESTS, FOR OUR LIVES DEPEND ON THEM'.

A TALE OF BOOKS

Shantanu was a very good student and he was in the sixth standard at school. Apart from studies, he was also good at sports and co-curricular activities. An avid reader, he had even read books from his mother's collection in his free time.

Seeing his love for reading books, his paternal grandfather had gifted him many good books. He really treasured these books and called them 'gems'. They comprised of a great assortment, ranging from subjects like science, geography, travel, history and even included many English classics.

Shantanu had a very regular and systematic daily routine. After getting home from school, he finished his homework and took a short nap. He went out to play with his friends in the evening and was expected to return home before dark, which he obediently did. After play he drank a glassful of milk in the evening.

Thereafter, he would go back to reading books. When he was busy reading books his mother often looked approvingly at him even when she was busy with the household chores. She often pointed out to him that 'A man is judged by the company he keeps and the books he reads'. She made sure that he always read the best of books suited for his age.

Shantanu always wanted to buy books of his own but with the limited income of his father he did not get a big sum of money as pocket money.

He was able to borrow many good books from his school library. But the 'one book a week' rule made by the strict librarian did not suit him. He had devised a clever way around this rule with his two very close friends; they borrowed one book each and each one of them read it quickly and circulated it amongst themselves within the week. Thus each of them got to read three books instead of one in a week. The librarian never got to know about it.

But as he was a voracious reader, he soon exhausted all his options to read more books from the school library. He longed to buy the books he really wanted to read.

The English teacher had recommended some good books which the students were expected to read during the summer vacation. Shantanu felt ill at ease because he had been able to read just a couple of them. He was constantly on the lookout for the titles which featured in the teacher's list.

Shantanu often visited a stationery shop nearby for his requirement of notebooks, pens, geometry instruments and colours etc. The shop owner was a young man named Vikas. Shantanu and Vikas got along very well and were close pals.

Whenever Shantanu visited Vikas's shop, the conversation inevitably turned to reading books. Vikas himself read many books in his free time. He had recommended some good books to Shantanu which he had tried to search for and borrow from his school library.

Although Shantanu got a small amount as pocket money yet he was able to save some of it for his urgent needs.

One day, he visited the stationery shop to buy poster colours and painting brushes. On reaching the shop he saw Vikas in a jubilant mood.

"Hello Vikas! You look very excited, what's the matter?" asked Shantanu curiously.

"Shantanu, I am so happy! I have acquired a new collection of English classics for sale" replied Vikas in an excited tone.

Shantanu was very pleased to hear that and he inquired, "Where are they? May I see them, please?"

"Sure! You deserve to be the first one to see them and have your pick first" Vikas said encouragingly.

Vikas led Shantanu to a new steel rack with many shelves placed behind the shop counter and gestured to him, "Here! All yours to see and to choose from! Let me know the ones you want to buy and I will offer you a reasonable price for them."

Shantanu was mesmerised to see the new hardbound books which stood immaculately arranged on the shelves. Vikas left him there to attend to some other customers. Shantanu got absorbed in reading all the titles which were on display. They formed an interesting collection of English classics and some books on travel and adventure.

He was overjoyed to see some of the titles which he longed for very much. There were some others which had been highly recommended by his school teacher. He selected a few titles which were: 'The Time Machine', '20,000 Leagues under the sea', 'Kidnapped', 'Treasure Island' and 'Travels of Marco Polo'.

Shantanu was reluctant to approach Vikas to ask the price of the books he had selected. He stood near the small pile of books he had selected and waited for Vikas to come to him instead.

Vikas saw Shantanu's uneasiness and approached him in a friendly manner. "What's the matter Shantanu, you look disturbed?" he asked.

"What's the price of these books?" Shantanu asked abruptly, pointing to the five books he had selected to buy.

Vikas smiled sympathetically as he had understood the cause of Shantanu's discomfort. He wanted to put Shantanu at ease and he replied very politely, "Not very expensive, just a hundred rupees apiece."

Shantanu looked somewhat relieved on hearing this and he mentally calculated the total price of the books he had selected to be rupees five hundred. He presently had only rupees two hundred with him.

He was in a dilemma as he wanted to take all the five books together. He was not sure Vikas would allow him to take all of them without making the full payment.

Vikas saw the hesitation in Shantanu's eyes and he asked immediately, "What's wrong now, you look confused?"

Shantanu replied reluctantly, "Vikas, to be honest I have just rupees two hundred with me right now. I had come to buy poster colours and painting brushes but now I want to buy these five books."

Vikas understood the whole situation. He looked at Shantanu with kindness and said, "We can work it out between ourselves. Don't worry too much."

"How's it possible? Shantanu asked with a look of amazement on his face.

Vikas explained patiently, "You can pay me rupees two hundred now and the balance you can pay in two instalments of rupees one hundred and fifty per month. For the sake of our friendship and your love for reading, that's the least I can do."

Before Shantanu could say anything, Vikas added, "I know I can trust you."

Shantanu could not believe his ears!

It was simply too good to be true. He felt relieved.

"Are you sure?" he asked anyway.

"Yes, positive" replied Vikas, beaming.

"Alright, it's a deal then. Here's rupees two hundred and the rest to be paid as agreed. I should be able to pay you from my pocket money" said Shantanu with finality.

Vikas put the books in a shopping bag and handed them to Shantanu and patted him on the back.

"Enjoy your reading and you can always come back for more" he said as Shantanu was hastily about to depart.

"Thank you! Thank you!" he shouted back.

Vikas smiled and waved to him. He continued to watch Shantanu go away and thought, "He is a true bibliophile and a good customer. I know I can trust him explicitly."

Shantanu walked as fast as his legs could carry him for he wanted to start reading the new books as soon as he got home. The poster colours and painting brushes were forgotten for now.

He was trying to figure out the reason for Vikas's trust in him. He gave it a long careful thought on his way home.

"It must be due to the fact that we share a common interest in reading books and we are very good friends" he thought, feeling good about the visit to Vikas's shop.

THE EMPEROR'S DILEMMA

We have all heard the saying "Uneasy lies the head that wears the crown." But there's another saying, albeit an unofficial one, that says "Uneasy rests the back that chairs the throne." Who can appreciate its true meaning more than Emperor 'Sher Bahadur' of 'Shergarh'! For, he had learnt it the 'hard' way.

In a dense jungle in Central India called 'Shergarh', a tiger called 'Sher Bahadur' once ruled over the other animals. He was very brave and certainly deserved the title 'Bahadur'. But at the same time, he was merciless, ferocious and whimsical.

All the animals big and small lived in terror of his wrath and cruelty. He was the acknowledged Emperor as, he had defeated many neighbouring kings in battle. All of whom now paid homage to him. He had thus come to rule over a very vast territory.

He was the master of his own whims and desires and all his subjects lived in utmost terror. Their lives were never safe as very minor mistakes and omissions made by them brought very harsh punishment and sometimes even death. Initially 'Sher Bahadur' had been hailed as a brave emperor but his arrogance, cruelty and ferocity had made him unpopular and notorious among his subjects.

None dared to annoy him for fear of what may befall them if anyone of the animals should become the object of the emperor's wrath. Some of the older animals had simply resigned themselves to their fate and did not bother about what future might hold for them.

'Sher Bahadur' used to hold court every week where he would seat himself on a 'throne' carved out of and situated on a high rock called the 'Raj Asana' and with the help of his trusted servants; hyenas and jackals, would discuss important matters and deliver his verdict which was binding on all.

Also it was the occasion to pronounce judgements on the offenders brought before him. The punishments meted out to them were severe in the least, ranging from flogging and even up to death sentence. The trusted jackals and hyenas who were also the emperor's advisors and friends were entrusted with the task of carrying out the sentences on the convicted offenders. They had a vested interest in being loyal to the emperor as they got the pickings from the leftovers of the emperor's meals and enjoyed a certain measure of power at the same time.

Over a period of time, migration of animals took place out of and into the domain of 'Sher Bahadur'. Some of his subjects moved to distant forests to avoid a cruel fate. Some new animals moved into 'Shergarh' from other areas in the hope of good food and shelter because here the jungle was the thickest and offered the best fruit trees and rich grazing grass.

The newcomers were mainly foxes, rabbits, crows and a few other birds. They had come from forests where the kings were liberal and benevolent and hence were not used to the harsh regime of 'Sher Bahadur'. They had led a carefree life there.

In 'Shergarh' however, they found the animals to be always scared, secretive and depressed; there was no happiness in the midst of plenty. The new arrivals initially could not understand the cause of the strange behaviour of the other animals but they were determined to find out for themselves.

One day in a meadow, a family of rabbits who were new to 'Shergarh' were running around playfully and eating some tender shoots when they sighted a herd of spotted deer coming out to the meadow from the dense forest beyond. They looked very tense and irritable and the stag who was the largest male in the herd and hence their head, stood guard at the edge of the jungle and allowed the females and fawns to go out to graze. As the herd grazed, every now and then they raised their heads and looked nervously towards the stag and to the jungle in the distance. The stag, in order to reassure them, in turn nodded to them and they continued to graze.

On seeing such a spectacle, the curiosity of the rabbits was aroused and they quietly approached the stag.

"O! Antlered beauty! Why do you look so sad and nervous?" asked the rabbits trying to strike a conversation with the stag.

"Why do you not graze with your herd and instead stand aloof looking so tense" they asked. The stag was surprised at being addressed in this manner but out of politeness he replied, "Thank you for the praise little ones but what good are these antlers if I cannot protect my herd from the emperor's wrath!"

"What do you mean?" asked the oldest rabbit.

The stag shook his big head and sighed. "Only a week ago the tiger, 'Sher Bahadur', killed one of my females and her fawn for no fault of theirs. Their only little mistake was that they did not bow properly as the emperor went past them in the forest. But that little omission was unintentional and understandable in the light of the fact that as the tiger passed close to them, the doe had been comforting the fawn who was very scared of the tiger. The two of them had thus become the target of the wrath of the emperor. They were summoned to the emperor's court and ordered to be killed. They were summarily dispatched by the jackals and hyenas and consumed then and there".

The rabbits listened with terrified faces and were speechless. They noticed tears rolling down the cheeks of the stag. None spoke for some moments.

Then the stag continued, "All the animals are at the mercy of the emperor who is very cruel and arrogant and terrorizes us all with acts of unprecedented cruelty and wanton killings."

"None is safe except his sycophants: the jackals and the hyenas, for they do all the dirty work for him. Similar fate has befallen many innocent animals but we have nowhere to go and none to turn to for help" said the stag with deep pain and sorrow in his voice.

The rabbits were deeply moved on hearing this sorrowful narrative. They had never thought that the reason for the strange behaviour of the animals was so sinister. They were themselves shivering with fear as they imagined the scenes of the emperor's cruelty.

With a heavy heart they comforted the stag with these words, "Big brother, nothing lasts forever. These days of sorrow and fear will soon be over."

"We shall talk to our friends and find a way to rid all the animals of 'Shergarh' of the menace of 'Sher Bahadur'.

"This is our promise to you. Now cheer up!" said the rabbits trying to handle the situation deftly.

"Thank you little ones! May God be with you and help us all" exclaimed the stag with moist eyes as he looked towards his grazing herd.

This strange incident had a deep impact on the minds of the rabbits who immediately rushed to where their friends the foxes and the crows were to be found.

They called out "Dear friends, please come quickly, we have learnt something dreadful!" The families of foxes and crows rushed to meet them.

The rabbits signaled for all of them to move discreetly to the denser part of the jungle for a serious conversation;

away from the eyes and out of earshot of the spies of the emperor; the lurking jackals and hyenas.

"The emperor is unjust and whimsical. He enjoys wanton killing and strikes terror into the hearts of his innocent subjects" blurted out the oldest rabbit as soon as they were in a safe area in the jungle. He then went on to describe his meeting with the stag and his herd earlier in the day. Everyone present was shocked to hear of such injustice and cruelty.

"What kind of a 'Bahadur' is he if he kills innocent and defenceless animals?" asked the head of the fox family.

"We do not accept him as our emperor and he must mend his ways" shouted the eldest of the clan of crows.

"Our families shall not live in fear and we refuse to be terrorized into subjugation" all the crows cawed in unison.

"But the big question is, what are we to do in order to put an end to this menace?" asked the fox.

"We are very few in numbers to stand up against 'Sher Bahadur' and all the other animals are weak and demoralised in spirit to even contemplate some action against the emperor" shouted the crow.

"Calm down! Calm down my dear friend and let me think awhile" requested the fox. He closed his eyes and the others waited anxiously for what he had to say.

The fox opened his eyes and looked straight ahead and said calmly, "We must send a representation to the emperor and point out that he must mend his ways or face the consequences."

"Aww! He's too arrogant to listen to such an appeal. After all that I have described to you about my meeting with the stag, we can very well see that there's not an iota of remorse or sense of justice in him. He is the incarnation of evil and must be tackled strongly" shouted the rabbit in a high voice.

The crow after having listened to the conversation, flapped his wings and said, "This problem will need a quick fix solution because we don't want to lose more of our friends."

"Yes I agree with him. As you can see, the rabbits and crows have a short life span and we don't want our children to grow up fearful for their lives. We wholeheartedly stand for a quick remedy to this menace" said the members of rabbit family.

"Alright, what do you suggest we do then?" asked the fox.

"I have a plan which can be best put into action by a lone animal. I shall do the needful myself if you all can entrust me with the job. We must be secretive and discreet" said the crow.

"We do trust you dear friend, but what are we to do in order to help you" asked all of them.

"Then just keep an eye on the daily routine of the emperor- like when he eats, sleeps, gets up, takes a bath and meets his coterie of friends etc. I think our friend the fox can be the spy to get all the relevant information and we can meet here again in a week's time" suggested the crow.

"Yes! Yes! We agree!" all of them shouted with glee.

So the fox became the spy and discreetly moved around in the jungle, keeping an eye on the movements and activities of the emperor. He made a careful mental note of all the activities of the emperor, the places he visited and the timings thereof, in order to accurately report back to the crow at the next meeting.

The next meeting was eagerly awaited as the plan formulated by the crow was to be revealed to them on that day.

So, the week went by and on the evening of the last day of the week all members of the previous meeting gathered at the predetermined place. When all had settled down, the fox disclosed all that she had gathered about the daily routine of the emperor, mainly for the benefit of the crow. Everyone listened with rapt attention. The crow carefully listened to all that was told and made a mental note of it. He closed his eyes for a while and thought deeply. He opened his eyes and they were shining with enthusiasm. He had inwardly come to a decision and had resolved to carry it out for the benefit of all the animals.

"I shall strike the emperor hard on his back side on an occasion of my choice and fly away" said the crow as a matter of fact.

"All of us can then spread the word of this outrage against the emperor by publicity and propaganda. This should produce the desired result and rid us and 'Shergarh' of 'Sher Bahadur' forever. He shall never be able to show his face in this jungle again" explained the crow with an air of anticipation.

"Bravo! Although it sounds risky but with God's grace victory shall be ours" shouted all the animals.

On the appointed day for the attack on the emperor, the crow got up early and looked out over the jungle from his nest high up in the tree and thought, "Today we shall launch our movement to be free from the tyrant."

He took a bath in a nearby pool and sharpened his beak on the branch of a tree and settled down to wait for afternoon. At noon he flew to a tree near the place where the tiger came for siesta after his meal. He did not have to wait long as the emperor walked into full view in a majestic and nonchalant manner.

The tiger looked around and yawned widely. Soon he settled down to sleep and began to snore loudly. The crow perched atop a nearby tree could see his whiskers vibrating in rhythm with his loud snores.

"Now is my big chance to strike!" thought the crow excitedly and swooped down at great speed and flew straight at the emperor. He now knew no fear of what may befall him. The welfare of all the animals was his sole concern and mission.

He flew as a 'kamikaze' pilot and struck the emperor with his sharp beak with terrific force.

The crow flew away immediately, even as the emperor growled violently in pain and surprise. "What the Hell! Who dare hit me? Whoever it was, will die a painful death at my hands" he snarled and shook his fists in anger.

The emperor was in great pain and the outrage against his authority had taken him by surprise. The crow meanwhile, had made good his escape and was nowhere to be seen. He flew to his nest hidden in the high branches of a tall tree. The emperor's cries of pain and frustration could be heard far and wide and all animals who were part of this conspiracy understood that the secret mission had been successfully carried out.

On hearing the tiger's cries of pain and anger the jackals and hyenas rushed to him to see what was wrong.

They saw the tiger limping about in pain and growling at the top of his voice repeating again and again, "Go, find the perpetrator of this attack on me! I shall tear him apart with my own claws and hang his skin out to dry! Go, go all of you and find him" he said at the top of his voice.

The hyenas and jackals were clueless as to the occurrence but in order to please the emperor, the leader of the pack of jackals took a closer look at the injury caused to the tiger. He shouted "Your Highness! The wound is really bad and is swollen and bleeding. We must call the Vaid before the pain becomes unbearable."

"Do as you please, call the Vaid immediately but once I am better that scoundrel who did this to me must die" grunted the tiger in frustration and pain.

The bear, who was the Vaid, was the royal doctor who practised the Ayurveda and lived some distance away in a cave. He was out collecting honey and some medicinal herbs for making medicaments, when he noticed a great commotion coming his way. He instantly recognised the emperor's 'dear' friends and straightened up from the task he was doing. Turning to the group that approached him, he asked sarcastically "What brings you here at this time of day, you should be enjoying your 'royal' meal by now (he meant the leftovers from the emperor's meal)?"

"The emperor has been attacked and is seriously wounded. Come quickly! He needs urgent medical attention" shouted the emperor's friends in unison.

The bear quickly gathered some essential medicaments into his bag and started for the emperor's dwelling. As the group reached about half the distance, they heard a loud husky voice singing faraway in the dense canopy of the trees; the words were:

"Ha! Ha! Ha! The emperor has a sore back,

For he was under an aerial attack,

O! He was struck when the crow could sneak,

And hit him with his sharp beak,

It was great fun,

To see the Emperor run"

The bear and the tiger's friends nodded their heads knowingly on hearing these words, now they could easily conclude that the premeditated attack on the emperor was the crow's doing.

"The emperor must be informed of this" said the hyenas.

"He will himself come to know soon" said the bear trying to hide his grin.

As the group moved farther they could see other animals in the jungle trying to catch the words of the crow's boastful song.

"This is not good for the emperor's pride and self-respect" thought the jackals and hyenas.

They reached the emperor's place shortly and found him in great suffering and agony. His anger had somewhat subsided. As the emperor was about to speak to the bear, he heard the crow singing some distance away. As he listened carefully, he could make out the words:

"The emperor has a sore back,

For he was under an aerial attack,

O! He was struck when the crow could sneak,

And hit him with his sharp beak,

It was great fun,

To see the Emperor run"

"Hmmm! So it was the crow who was bold enough to attack me: 'Sher Bahadur'" said the tiger as the sarcasm of the words became clear to him.

"Let me just get better and I will show him the stuff I am made of" he said to none in particular and more as a means to give vent to his frustration.

"Now, if you will please let me examine your wound, Your Highness!" said the bear courteously.

'Sher Bahadur' acceded to the Vaid's request and lay down in prone position on a mat of grass. The bear made a quick examination of the tiger's wound and straightened up.

"How bad is it?" asked the emperor as he himself sat upright in a painful manner.

"It is a deep wound which will take many days to heal. The pain and swelling will take a week to subside" said the bear.

He brought out some herbs from his bag and mixed them with herbal oil to make a poultice which he gently patted into place over the wound. "This should stay in place for a week and the wound will heal fast and in case I am needed, please send word and your loyal servant shall be at your service your Majesty" said the bear in a most courteous and respectful manner.

"OK, I will let you know how I feel in a couple of days" said the emperor and dismissed the bear.

He then turned to the jackals and hyenas who had been standing quietly nearby and said, "You may leave now, I need to rest."

He lay down as the hyenas and jackals went away casting anxious glances towards him. After a little rest the pain in the wound eased slightly and he dozed off.

He was soon awake. He had been disturbed by the loud singing of the crows which was clearly audible and had been joined by other birds.

He could see that many animals on the ground were also keeping the beat of the rhythm by stomping their feet. This spectacle was very unsettling for 'Sher Bahadur', who saw it as an act of defiance, almost a revolt against his authority and rule.

The emperor knew no peace of mind after this incident for he knew that almost all animals in his domain knew of the daring attack on him by the crow and had been emboldened by it. They were now in open defiance to his authority as they had found unity in numbers.

The day after the attack, as the emperor limped about in search of a meal, he could hear some giggling noises in the bushes.

On getting closer he could hear the herd of deer say to their young ones "Get away all of you! Here comes His Highness: the Limping Tiger!"

The tiger was struck by the audacity of the deer and felt humiliated. "I am unable to hunt and am starving" he said to himself.

"In this condition I have become the butt of their jokes, all animals big and small are poking fun at me" he grumbled as he made his way to meet his trusted servants.

The jackals and hyenas had a look of deep concern in their eyes as they welcomed the tiger in their midst. He seated himself on a comfortable patch of soft grass and his body language was not very positive.

The hyenas tried to cheer him up by saying "Your Highness! You will get well soon. This is just a temporary phase and will soon pass and the wound will heal. Then we can teach each one of them a lesson for their insolence."

"Your Highness! Shall we bring you something to eat" said the jackals not to be outdone in flattering the emperor.

On hearing this, the tiger screwed up his nose and made an unpleasant face and shouted, "NO! Not the stuff you are used to eating. You are now making me angry with your silly words! Go away all of you and let me rest! I need to do some serious thinking."

The jackals and hyenas slipped away quietly for fear of annoying the tiger.

The tiger stretched himself to rest and to plan for his future in the light of the recent developments in his domain. As he lay there dejected and frustrated, nursing his injured back side and his shattered ego and self-respect, he could hear the faraway singing of the crows as they flew away to their homes.

The words were all too familiar to him now. He tried to cover his ears to shut out the sound which now haunted him, making his life miserable.

He was in a dilemma for he wanted to preserve the last remnants of his self-esteem. He needed to think clearly and plan carefully.

"I have become the laughing-stock of all the beasts of the jungle. My authority and respect have been shattered. How can I ever face these animals again! The wound on my back will heal but the blot on my self-respect cannot be erased. I shall never regain the same authority and status that I have enjoyed in the past. It will be very good for me to move away silently to some other forest rather than be disgracefully thrown out of' Shergarh" thought 'Sher Bahadur' at length.

He simply lay there gloomily and waited for darkness to descend when he would quietly slip away from the jungle. He planned to travel by the secret trail that went past the stream at the outer edge of the forest. He would thus be able to avoid all detection and be safely away by daybreak.

At dusk, the emperor roused himself and secretly limped away from his beloved domain where he had ruled with impunity for so long and had been the master of his will.

The throne he had sat upon; the 'Raj Asana' had suddenly become very uncomfortable to sit upon. It was manifest destiny and he had to accept his fate with his head bowed down.

"Perhaps it was too good to last forever" he thought as he took one last look around and stealthily took to the trail past the stream. He did not even bother to say goodbye to his ever loyal jackals and hyenas.

Unbeknownst to the tiger, a lone sentry on a tree top sighted him and flew away to inform his friends.

He was just a 'lowly crow' and he carried the good news of their freedom from the tyrannical emperor; 'Sher Bahadur'.

A PACKET OF SWEETS

Sukhbir Singh had decided to move to Delhi from Punjab. He had got a new job as a sales representative of a machine tools company. The salary offered was good and shifting to Delhi had always been his keen desire. The company had its office in Kashmere Gate market. His wife, Amanpreet, had enthusiastically approved of his decision, having in mind the best interest of their two sons; Samar aged three years and Amar aged one year.

Sukhbir and his wife looked forward to a good standard of living in Delhi. They wanted to provide a good education to their two sons and enable them to grow up as responsible citizens of the country; Delhi seemed an ideal place for them to realize their vision. In the process, their sons would also have a good opportunity to stand firmly on their feet and carve out a niche for themselves in the competitive world, so they thought.

Sukhbir had joined his new workplace and when he got off from work, he went looking for a suitable accommodation for his family in the nearby area. In the meantime, they were staying in a guesthouse near his office. The household goods and furniture etc. were to arrive in a few days by road transport. He really needed to find a suitable accommodation for his family at the earliest.

One day he had a talk about this with his colleague Suresh, who promised to help him in his search for a suitable accommodation. In a couple of days he received a favourable response from Suresh. He went and announced to his wife, "There's a two-bedroom apartment at Model Town which we can rent. The owner is known to my colleague in the new company."

"Sounds great!" exclaimed Amanpreet.

"When can we go there and see the accommodation?" she asked.

"We shall all go there tomorrow morning. Since it's a Sunday, we can spend some time there and see the locality as well. I have heard a lot of praise about it and I hope you will like it" answered Sukhbir.

Amanpreet nodded in agreement.

"Model Town sounds good to me but what about the rent?" she inquired.

"My colleague Suresh has assured me that he will talk to the owner and bring it down to a reasonable amount. You don't have to worry." said Sukhbir trying to put his wife at ease.

Next morning they got ready after breakfast and left for Model town in a hired taxi. After a drive of about four kilometers they reached Model Town. They located the proper address and knocked at the gate.

The gate was opened by a Gurkha guard. He welcomed them with a broad grin which showed his tobacco-stained teeth.

"Jai Hind! Sahib! I am Ram Bahadur; chowkidar and caretaker" he said standing in 'Attention': military style. He ushered them to the apartment on the ground floor which was to let.

"Were you expecting us?" Sukhbir asked, amazed at the friendliness of the guard.

"Ji, Sahib, Sureshji had instructed me to help you" said Ram Bahadur as he unlocked the rooms for them.

Ram Bahadur had been the guard at the house for the past five years and after the previous tenant of the apartment had vacated the place six months earlier, he had been very lonely. He was thus looking forward to good company. He had taken a fancy for Sukhbir and his family and really liked their small boys who reminded him of his own children in Nepal.

After having a good look around the place, Sukhbir conferred with his wife about her opinion of the accommodation.

Ram Bahadur stood at a respectful distance and waited anxiously for their decision.

"Ram Bahadur, we shall take a short walk in the locality and will be back shortly" Sukhbir told him.

Ram Bahadur nodded emphatically on hearing these words.

Sukhbir took Samar by the hand and Amanpreet carried Amar on her arm and they left the place. They walked along the main street and saw that the colony looked very neat and serene. The pavements along the roadside were clean and shady trees spread their branches to provide cool shade all along the road.

As they walked along for some distance, they came to a well-constructed house which displayed a large signboard 'PLAYWAY SCHOOL'.

Sukhbir stopped suddenly on reading the signboard and a thought flashed through his mind!"My sons can get started with their education here" he thought. He moved closer to the boundary wall to get a better look inside the school which was closed (the day being a Sunday).

He saw the swings and the see-saw in the lawn which was neat and tidy. Further away he saw the classrooms.

His wife moved closer to him and whispered, "I know what you are thinking."

Sukhbir looked at her in surprise and smiled affectionately. Meanwhile, Samar had been watching the place with keen interest and he suddenly exclaimed, "My school, my school!" His parents burst out laughing and Amar too smiled broadly in his childish way.

Shortly thereafter, they made their way back to the house, their mind firmly made up. On reaching the place, Sukhbir summoned Ram Bahadur, who came running.

"Ram Bahadur, you can inform your employer that we will rent this place. We will be ready to move here in a few days" Sukhbir told him.

"Ji, Sahib!" he said and saluted them.

Sukhbir and his family started planning about moving to the apartment in Model Town after returning to the guesthouse. The household goods and furniture arrived in a big truck a few days later and Sukhbir directed them to be unloaded at the rented apartment. The family moved to the apartment to arrange things and get settled in the new accommodation. They were able to set up things in a day's time and were thankful to Ram Bahadur for his wholehearted help.

The new home was very comfortable and convenient for them. Sukhbir could easily travel to his workplace. The local market was nearby and the school too; O! The school!

Suddenly one day, Amanpreet remembered that Samar had to be admitted to the school. She spoke to her husband that very evening when he returned home. Samar overheard their conversation and he came and stood next to his father. He held his father's hand and looked at him directly. He said, "Papa, I will go and join the school only if you take me there." Samar's parents were surprised at

Samar's display of emotions and suddenly he hugged his father and said, "You are the best papa in the whole world and I love you very much." His parents smiled at him affectionately.

Next day, Sukhbir and Amanpreet took Samar to the 'PLAYWAY SCHOOL'. Amar went with them too.

They met the Principal, Mrs. Mathur, in her office. She asked Samar a few basic questions and enrolled him to the pre-nursery class. Samar's parents completed the small formalities of documentation and paid the fees. They returned home thereafter.

Samar had to attend school for five days a week from 9 AM to 12 AM. The teaching programme at the school was carefully designed to make the students interested in learning, in a light and playful manner.

Samar's class teacher, Ms. Anita, was responsible for teaching the class and also for engaging and guiding them in co-curricular activities. Mrs. Mathur, the Principal, was incidentally also the founder of the school. She took a great interest in the school and sometimes came by to see that things were going as scheduled.

Samar was an intelligent and active student who took great interest in learning and sports. He was always very anxious to go to school. He had befriended all the children in his class. When he came home after school, he narrated his experiences of the day to his mother earnestly.

Since the school was just a short distance away from their residence, his mother would take him to school every morning and fetch him back when the school got over in the afternoon.

One day, it was Samar's classmate, Sharad's birthday. Sharad's parents had left small packets of assorted sweets with Ms. Anita, to be distributed among the children.

The class teacher took the roll call and thereafter she asked every student to stand up when their name was called. She gave each of them a packet of the birthday sweets.

When she called out Samar's name, he stood up smartly to collect his packet of sweets. Instead, the teacher said, "Samar! You are very naughty and I will not give you the sweets."

Samar was dumbstruck! He stood there shocked at the teacher's words. He felt humiliated in front of the whole class. All his class mates around him started giggling. He held back his tears with great effort. But he soon recovered himself and before the teacher could move on to the next student, he stood upright and said boldly, "Ma'am, I don't need these sweets. I can get all the sweets I need from my father." After saying so, he sat down and avoided eye contact with the teacher. The teacher was surprised on hearing these words from a young boy and her face wore a blank look.

Soon the class got over and Samar went out to play with his friends and he ignored the incident. When the school got over, he rushed to the main gate of the school to meet his mother. On seeing him, his mother came inside to collect his bag and she lovingly caressed his head. They were about to start for home when, Ms. Anita called Samar by name. They stopped and turned around and saw her making her way towards them. She came to them and tried to press the packet of sweets into Samar's hands with the words, "This is for you." Samar instantly pushed away the sweets and moved closer to his mother.

The teacher looked at Amanpreet and said imploringly, "Please give these sweets to Samar." With these words she handed the packet of sweets to Samar's mother.

Samar was very happy to be home as usual and happily played with his younger brother. In the evening his mother tried to give him the packet of sweets but he bluntly refused even to touch them. Amanpreet was very surprised at her son's unusual behaviour for he was otherwise fond of sweets. She was able to make Samar narrate the whole incident to her at length, as it had transpired at school that day.

When Sukhbir came home in the evening, his wife served him tea and went and sat next to him. When he had finished his cup of tea, he took out a packet of toffees from his bag and handed them to his wife.

"These are for Samar and Amar. Where are they?" he asked as he looked around for his sons. He called Samar, who came running and hugged his father. "My dear son, these are for you and your brother, go and enjoy yourself" he said handing him the packet of toffees. Samar looked in amazement at the packet of sweets and then at his father. "That's great, thank you, papa" he said and ran away to where Amar was playing. He went and shared the sweets with his brother amidst a lot of laughter. The boys continued to play excitedly.

After these brief moments of affection with his son, Sukhbir turned to his wife. He could see that she wanted to speak to him and she looked very serious.

Amanpreet spoke to him about the incident at school as Samar had described it to her.

Suhhbir was in deep thought after hearing the entire incident. His wife looked at him and patiently waited for him to speak.

After a long silence, Sukhbir shook his head understandingly and said to his wife, "As I see it, Samar has a deep sense of self-respect and the teacher inadvertently wounded his self-respect with her careless words. Samar deserves all our love and understanding, for even at this tender age he has a strong character. He is self-sufficient and is not lured by material things. We should be proud of our son."

"He is very right in expecting his parents to fulfill his needs" said Sukhbir very proudly.

"You have analyzed his behaviour very simply but I think he may have been egoistic in the whole affair"

Amanpreet said uncertainly as she continued the conversation.

Her husband looked at her appreciatively and replied, "No! I don't think so. If it had been his ego, he would have accepted the sweets from his teacher when the school got over, with a sense of victory. But he has been quite detached and the whole incident was very uncomfortable for him."

"Such strong character is rarely seen in someone so young and we must also admire him for his unshakeable trust in his parents" he added.

Amanpreet listened patiently and on careful thinking, she wholeheartedly agreed with her husband. Deep inside, she too, felt very proud of her son.

HONESTY IS THE BEST POLICY

Amitabh excitedly looked out of the window of his train compartment as the Kalka Mail approached the outskirts of Howrah. The Asansol and Burdwan stations had already gone by and Howrah was the final destination of the train. Amitabh was travelling to Howrah and on to Kolkata.

Howrah is situated on the right bank of the River Hooghly which is a distributary of the mighty Ganges. Kolkata is on the left bank of the River Hooghly. One has to cross over the Howrah Bridge from Howrah when going to Kolkata.

The journey by train, which had begun on the morning of the day before, from Delhi Junction was about to end after 22 hours of overnight travel at Howrah Junction. Amitabh could hardly wait to be in the city where he had enjoyed himself so much during the winter vacations for so many years regularly along with his mother and younger brother. He had fond memories of those visits to Kolkata when in the past he had visited his maternal grandfather and his family.

Amitabh was now going to Kolkata as a sales representative of a big book publishing house in New

Delhi. He was very excited to visit the city after a gap of over twenty five years.

His grandfather had died many years ago and his maternal uncles had moved to their native village with their families thereafter. So, he had basically lost touch with the 'City of Joy'.

He had purposely taken the Kalka Mail, although faster trains were available for Howrah. The Kalka Mail started from Delhi at around 8 AM and during the course of the journey of about 1500 kilometers it travelled through three States and a Union territory of India. This allowed him a lot of sight-seeing in daytime. Amitabh was thus able to relive the experiences of his childhood days on seeing some of the once familiar sites. Although with time, all the places had been transformed considerably.

Among the favourite sites that he could see during the journey was the Bamrauli Air Force Station near Allahabad (now called Prayagraj) which is the HQ of the Central Air Command of the IAF. It was here that his younger brother and he had always tried to see the famous MiG-21 aircraft (nicknamed 'Bison') of the IAF, parked in their hangars as the train passed close to the Air base.

He saw that it had now been upgraded to serve as a modern domestic airport. (Soon it will be developed into an international airport.) Other places of interest to him were the Mughalsarai (now Deendayal Upadhyay) station where he drank fresh hot milk just as his brother and he had done in their younger days and the famous 'Jawahar

Setu' which spanned for several kilometers over the river Sone at the city of Dehri-on-Sone, at night.

He had been filled with nostalgia and really missed his mother and brother.

Now he looked forward to the end of his journey. It was 6 AM in the morning and broad daylight when the train chugged into the station, for Howrah is in West Bengal in eastern India where the sun rises early. Amitabh could see the bright sun shining through the iconic HOWRAH BRIDGE. This bridge was commissioned in 1943. Tata Iron and Steel Company had supplied 23,500 tonnes of specified high grade steel required for the construction of this bridge. This bridge has stood strong for nearly 80 years now.

Amitabh got out of the train as soon as it came to a halt. He carried his handbag, which was his only item of luggage and quickly walked to the exit to hail a taxi cab. On reaching outside the station, he saw that all the taxis were lined up in an orderly manner and their drivers stood alongside each of them. He approached the one nearest to him and asked, "Which taxi will take me to Lindsay Street?"

He had booked a room for two days at an economy hotel on Lindsay Street near the New Market in South Kolkata. This would allow him to conveniently visit the bookstores nearby on Park Street and Lord Sinha Road.

The taxi driver very politely greeted him. "Babuji, we are lined up here, turn wise. The very first taxi in this long line will take the passengers first. This is our mutually acceptable arrangement" he told Amitabh.

"OK, Thanks, I shall go to him" said Amitabh as he hurried to the first taxi in the line. He saw a couple with a small child already walking towards it. He managed to reach it first.

The taxi driver was leaning on the left front door, reading the morning newspaper. He was a middle aged tall Sikh with a flowing beard and thick moustache. He was neatly dressed in light grey trousers and white shirt and was wearing a dark blue turban.

Amitabh spoke immediately as the driver came over to him, "Take me to Lindsay Street. How much will you charge?" he said. The driver courteously folded his hands and greeted Amitabh, "Sat Siri Akal" he said. (It is the customary greeting of the Sikhs).

"Welcome to Kolkata, Babuji. You can pay the fare as per the meter and add rupees twenty for the increased fuel prices" he replied and came forward and opened the door for Amitabh to get in the rear passenger seat. He took his handbag and placed it next to Amitabh when he was seated.

The driver went around the taxi and got in the driver's seat and adjusted the rear view mirror and put the taxi in forward motion. Amitabh had observed with great wonder that the yellow Ambassador diesel-run taxis had not been decommissioned in Kolkata and now he was riding in one!

Amitabh found the taxi to be very neat and comfortable. There was a picture of Guru Nanak, the first Sikh guru on the dashboard and Gurbani (recitation from the Sikh scriptures) was playing on the sound system.

Amitabh couldn't stop himself from exclaiming, "I see that you are a Sikh and a very pious man!" "What's your name?" he asked.

"I am Surjeet Singh" the driver replied haltingly, evidently unaccustomed to much conversation with the passengers.

"Babuji are you coming to Kolkata for the first time" Surjeet Singh asked Amitabh.

"No, I used to come here every year during Christmas vacations to visit my Nanaji (maternal grandfather) and I was here last in 1992 when the new bridge over the Hooghly, 'Vidyasagar Setu' was inaugurated" replied Amitabh.

He somehow liked the mild-mannered Sikh driver and asked him, "How about you? Where are you from?"

Surjeet Singh was concentrating on driving as they were passing through some heavy traffic. They halted at the traffic lights and when the lights turned green the driver eased the taxi forward. Thereafter he replied,

"My grandfather had come to Kolkata from Ludhiana, in Punjab, about 50 years ago, looking for a better life."

"I see! What did he do here?" asked Amitabh expressing his keen interest.

"What I am doing right now, drive a taxi" Surjeet Singh chuckled.

"The big difference, however, is that he rented a taxi from the owner for a fixed amount per day and worked for 15 hours each day to make a living and I am fortunate enough to own this taxi and work as I please" said the driver in a confident voice.

"Did he make enough money?' asked Amitabh, evidently interested to know more about the life of Surjeet's grandfather.

"Yes! But, not too soon. He lived in a dormitory and led a simple life to save enough money to bring his family to Kolkata. After about two years, his wife and two sons were able to join him in Kolkata. They had started living in a two-room rented accommodation. The family life had always suited my grandfather and he once more began to enjoy the comforts of family life such as home-cooked food, comfortable and neat bed and the company of his loved ones" said Surjeet with a smile as he recalled what he had been told as a child by his father.

"He must have been a very hard-working man!" Amitabh remarked.

"Yes Babuji. He even gave his sons a decent education and when they were grown up, he bought a new taxi each for both of them and set them up in the transport business. The elder of his sons was my father" said the driver.

"Did your grandfather save enough money to buy the two new taxis or did he raise a loan for the purpose" asked Amitabh curiously.

Surjeet Singh was encouraged to speak at length by Amitabh's interest and attentiveness in what he was saying. He continued, "He took a loan from a private financier at a high rate of interest, as in those days there were no easy Business loans or Car loans. But he worked hard along with his two sons and they were able to pay the instalments of the loan amount on time" explained Surjeet.

"I can see that you are carrying on the family business admirably" Amitabh said with appreciation.

Surjeet Singh's voice suddenly took on a serious tone, and he said to Amitabh, "Babuji, it was my grandfather's honesty which was a great blessing for the entire family and even today we remember him and admire him for his good qualities of head and heart."

"Wow! That sounds very interesting, please tell me all about it" Amitabh said curiously.

"Babuji, we are very close to our destination now and I will tell you briefly about it. I suggest, we first stop at 'K. C. Das Sweets' at Esplanade. There you can try some authentic Bengali sweets, no fun coming to Kolkata and not tasting the famous 'rossogulla' and 'sondes' at this place" Surjeet suggested as he turned towards the famous sweets shop and halted.

"You can go in and order for yourself while I wait here for you, but please be quick about it as this is a 'NO PARKING' Zone" he said.

Amitabh nodded understandingly and alighted from the taxi and quickly went into the shop. He soon came out with a satisfied look on his face. He carried two small packages and he handed one to Surjeet and said, "This is for you, your suggestion was wonderful!"

Surjeet accepted the packet containing 'sondes' with a little hesitation and as Amitabh got in; he put the taxi in motion. He was keen to complete his narrative and spoke again, "The records of the loan including the repayment etc. were maintained manually in a ledger (as there were no computers at that time) at the financier's office and my grandfather had his copy of the records in a small passbook. Many other people had borrowed money from the same financier for various purposes" he said.

"One day a great tragedy occurred at the financier's office. There was a devastating fire and the entire place was burnt down. Many of the members of staff had suffered burn injuries. All the records and ledgers were destroyed in this fire. The financier was ruined as he had no way to claim repayment of loans and almost all the borrowers simply vanished. Others intentionally hid their passbooks so as to avoid paying back the borrowed amount. But my grandfather was a very honest man and he had approached the financier and expressed his deep sorrow at the tragedy. He had dutifully produced his passbooks which showed the amount due to the financier. The financier had been amazed at his honest deed and he had tearfully embraced my grandfather. As a gesture of goodwill and appreciation he had waived the interest on the loan amount and had even allowed him to repay the amount in very easy instalments" Surjeet explained to Amitabh who sat amazed at the narrative.

"That was the big turning point in my family's fortune as the same financier wholeheartedly financed our family business for all times to come, and on very favourable terms. My father and his brother were able to expand the transport business and my grandfather was only too glad to retire from work. He died many years ago, when I was a child, but he lived to see the day when his sons had honestly carved out a niche for themselves and made his dream a reality. We now own a fleet of taxis and luxury cars and are very well off," Surjeet Singh said proudly.

"Surjeet, your grandfather was a noble soul and a true pioneer. Such qualities are rarely seen in men" Amitabh said admiringly. Surjeet Singh swelled with pride and sat a little straighter for that. It was evident that he was proud of his heritage.

They had now turned the corner into the Lindsay Street and Surjeet Singh located Amitabh's hotel and stopped in front of it. "Here you are, Babuji, we have arrived" he informed.

"Yes! Thank you for the lovely drive and the inspiring story about your grandfather. Honesty is the best policy, after all" said Amitabh looking at Surjeet and he warmly shook hands with him.

"Babuji, honesty is the best policy for all generations" he replied laughing and handed his visiting card to Amitabh.

Amitabh paid him the fare along with a tip, looked at the card and put it in his pocket. 'GURU NANAK TRAVELS' it said.

Surjeet respectfully thanked Amitabh on being paid his fare along with a generous tip. He said "If you are in Kolkata again and need my services, please feel free to give me a call, SAT SIRI AKAL!"

He departed immediately as Amitabh moved into the hotel carrying his handbag. He was making entries into the Customer register at the Reception of the hotel, when he saw Surjeet walking towards him. He couldn't quite comprehend the scenario. He waited for him to come up to him.

Surjeet came and stopped next to him. He extended his open palm towards him and Amitabh saw that in it lay his expensive mobile phone. Before he could react, Surjeet spoke up, "Babuji, you forgot this on your seat." And so doing, he handed the phone to its rightful owner.

Amitabh recovered himself and shook hands with him and thanked him. He was at a loss for words.

"That's quite remarkable. You practise what you preach! That's good Karma" was all he could manage to say to Surjeet Singh.

THE WATER BOTTLE

Samar and Amar were two brothers. Samar was elder to Amar by two years. They studied in the same school. Samar was in class 5 and Amar in was in class 3. Samar took good care of his younger brother while at school.

At school, during the recess, the bigger boys often crowded at the water taps and the younger ones were denied a chance to quench their thirst.

Amar faced a similar situation occasionally and often grumbled about it to his elder brother.

"Samar, I feel so thirsty during lunch break but I don't get to drink water as the bigger boys crowd around the taps. It is so frustrating" he said one day, choking back tears of dismay.

Samar consoled him and said, "I will tell mummy to buy you a water bottle."

Samar's words of understanding and affection brought an instant glow to Amar's sad face. He said with a broad grin "Sure! Please do tell her that, I really need it."

They got back from school and after having finished lunch, Amar nudged Samar in his ribs, prompting him to talk to their mother about buying a water bottle for him.

Samar immediately spoke up. "Mummy" he said, "The bigger boys at school are very inconsiderate and don't give the younger boys a chance to drink cool water from the taps. Amar too is facing the same problem."

"Hmm! What can be done about it? Shall I speak to the school authorities about this problem?" she asked gently. Her tone of voice reflected her concern for Amar.

"Why can't you buy me a water bottle to carry drinking water to school!" said Amar, speaking confidently for himself.

"Yes! I will do just that. You come with me to the market in the evening and choose a water bottle for yourself" said his mother decidedly.

Amar was pleased at the outcome of the brief discussion. He was surprised at the same time at how willingly his mother had agreed to meet his demand. He could only understand it as his mother's love and affection for him, flowing through her loving gesture.

In the evening, he hopped along merrily with his mother to the market and they returned shortly afterwards with Amar proudly carrying a new water bottle in a wrapper. He unwrapped it and showed it to Samar.

He said excitedly, "See brother! I have this new water bottle. Now, even you can be sure of getting cool water to drink at school".

His simple statement full of love and affection for his elder brother brought a smile to Samar's face. He was very pleased and said lovingly, "Yes dear, I know. Thank you!"

The new water bottle was dark green in colour and had a capacity of 2 litres of water. It had a brown plastic shoulder strap for ease of carrying it and a screw-on cap with a plastic stopper inside the cap.

Amar was very fond of his new water bottle and carried it to school daily. His water problem had been solved!

Even when at home, he often kept his water bottle in the refrigerator and drank water from it.

One day the two brothers were at home and their mother had gone to the market to buy some provisions.

Amar opened the refrigerator casually and holding the door open, he pulled out his water bottle. He unscrewed the cap and put the bottle to his lips and drank water from it in big gulps.

Samar was sitting at a table nearby and reading a new Hardy Boys novel. Suddenly Amar began to cough and sputter and the bottle fell from his hands, spilling water.

"What's the matter with you? Can't you drink slowly" shouted Samar visibly disturbed and irritated by the commotion caused by Amar.

Amar did not answer and merely pointed to his throat with a limp hand. Samar immediately shot out from his seat and lunged forward towards Amar. He could think of nothing except that something was stuck in Amar's throat and was choking him.

Samar cupped his right hand and slammed it hard onto the back of Amar's neck!

The impact of his blow was strong and sudden! Amar was thrown forwards and the plastic stopper of the bottle popped out of his mouth and flew away. Amar coughed violently and spat saliva and water onto the floor. He was breathing rapidly and deeply.

Slowly his breathing returned to normal and he looked around to see Samar standing close by, looking anxiously at him. He hugged his elder brother tightly.

They stood there for some minutes. Amar released his hold and Samar led him to the bed. They sat down side by side on the bed.

When Amar was able to talk coherently, he explained the cause of the unpleasant incident. He said, "Samar, the stopper of the bottle had somehow fallen in and when I took a big gulp of water it got lodged in my throat and choked me. Your presence of mind and timely intervention saved my life today."

Samar pulled Amar close to him and put his arm around him.

As they sat there, Samar began to sob suddenly and hugged Amar tightly.

They recovered themselves and started to think whether to tell their mother about this unpleasant incident or not. They were in a dilemma because a firm scolding was a definite possibility.

When their mother returned home, they approached her with downcast eyes. She was quick to notice that something was amiss.

"What's wrong? Have you two been quarrelling?" she asked.

Samar spoke first and narrated the incident to her. She was shocked to hear of the near death experience Amar had had but she patted Samar on the back and said "Well done boy! You saved your brother's life, I am proud of you."

And so saying, she pulled Samar closer by his shirtfront and hugged him. Tears of relief and joy rolled down her cheeks onto Samar's neck.

Samar looked up at her. Amar, on seeing them together in that way, came forward and huddled the two of them. They stayed in the same manner for some minutes, feeling the joy of togetherness. They were immensely relieved that things had not taken an ugly turn that afternoon.

THE MYSTERIOUS SHOEPRINT

Sukhbir Singh had moved to Delhi some years ago from Punjab. He had a job in Delhi. He stayed in a rented two-bedroom apartment in Model Town. His two sons Samar and Amar were now seven and five years old respectively. Since their age difference was so small, the two brothers were good companions and great pals.

They were very much alike in appearance but their habits and behaviour were very different from each other.

Amanpreet, their mother took very good care of them. She was largely responsible for their education as well. She also inculcated many virtues in her sons which she thought would stand them in good stead in their lives.

The two brothers went to a good public school that was close to their place of residence. They liked going to school, although for different reasons. Samar was a devoted and serious student whereas Amar was more easy-going and fun-loving. Going to school for him was an opportunity to play with friends.

Amar's parents were not overly concerned about his attitude and would remark occasionally, "He is a good boy and will emulate his elder brother. He is playful due to his age."

Amanpreet sent them to school neatly dressed everyday but on their return, the two boys were a study in contrast.

Samar always came back home neat and tidy.

But Amar! Oh! He was in a dishevelled condition. His shirt was always out of his shorts, shoelaces were loose and undone (with one or both of them missing sometimes) and the shoes were always covered in dust.

Samar always carried his schoolbag smartly whereas Amar threw his bag down from the steps of the school bus for his mother to carry. He himself would in turn, jump down from the highest point of the footboard of the school bus instead of stepping down.

"Amar please stop it! You will get hurt!" his mother would exclaim on several occasions and shake her head in disbelief.

She put up with Amar's carefree and playful attitude with great patience even as she rushed him home for a bath and change of clothes every day before serving him lunch. Amar enjoyed being playful and naughty.

Being the youngest in the family, he was the favourite and beloved. He often giggled sheepishly on seeing the look of disapproval on his mother's face.

One such day, when the boys returned from school, a strange thing happened!

Amanpreet noticed a muddy shoeprint on the front of Amar's shirt. He was quite oblivious to it and walked home unabashedly in his usual playful manner. His mother said nothing about the shoeprint in the most unexpected place.

"I will not bring up this point right now" she had thought.

"Let the boys finish their lunch first, then I shall ask Amar by taking him aside. Let him come out with the truth" she decided.

Samar and Amar soon finished their lunch and praised their mother's culinary skills. Samar walked away to his bedroom for the afternoon nap. Amar was about to join his brother when his mother summoned him to her.

Amar looked towards her and walked slowly up to her. She was seated in an easy chair and could very well see the look of uncertainty on Amar's face on being unexpectedly called by her. Nevertheless, he gathered some courage and approached her. "What is it, mummy? Why have you called me?" he asked.

"Please come and sit next to me, I want to ask you something" said Amanpreet.

As Amar came and sat next to her, she tried to put him at ease and said, "Amar, you are a good boy. I expect you to tell me the truth."

"Yes mummy, but what is it about? Amar asked affectionately.

"Please tell me all that you know about the dirty shoeprint on the front of your school shirt" she inquired softly.

Amar pretended to be surprised on hearing this. He knew he could not lie to his mother but he tried, nevertheless. He put on an innocent look and said "What shoeprint! Mummy I didn't notice any."

"Do you want me to show you the shirt?" asked his mother in a firm voice. A moment later she got up from the chair and brought his school shirt and put it in front of him to see.

"Here! Now take a look and tell me what you can recall about this shoeprint. Beware! For if you lie to me, I shall go and see your class teacher about it" she warned him.

Amar's face had a sullen look, for he knew his game was up. He was just playing for time to think of a convincing reason for the whole thing.

Amanpreet was impatient and she again pointed to the shirt and said, "You see this, this is the shoeprint I am talking about."

Amar thought quickly and after a brief pause, he answered, "Mummy, you see our school ground is very muddy after the recent rains. I was running fast during the games period and while striding I must have hit myself with my own foot. This is how my own shoeprint happens to be on my shirt front."

He looked sheepishly at his mother, knowing fully well that such an excuse may not be enough to convince her. He knew his mother hated lies.

Amanpreet was astounded at Amar's reply but she smiled inwardly at her son's witty answer.

"Amar, can you show me the manner in which you were running so as to be able to hit yourself with your own foot and leave a shoeprint on the front of your own shirt?" she asked him firmly.

Amar was now speechless but he tried many different running positions so as to hit himself on the front of his shirt with his own foot. All his efforts to this end amused his mother.

Finally, exhausted, he gave up trying and stood in front of his mother with his head lowered. She pulled him close and spoke very distinctly, "I know that you have been in a fight and one of the boys has kicked you on your chest. That's how the shoeprint happens to be there."

She scolded him for not telling the truth. "You could have been seriously hurt, I need to bring this to the notice of the school authorities" she said firmly.

Amar was terrified! He knew that he could not lie in front of his teachers. He started crying and tearfully he hugged his mother.

"Mummy I wanted to tell you the truth but I was scared that you will be very annoyed with me" he sobbed.

"Please forgive me, I shall not lie again. But the truth is that I did not fight with anyone or get kicked in a fight. It was meant to be a prank which my friends thought of and they deliberately made the shoeprint on my shirt" he said.

"Are you telling the truth now? Can I believe you?" his mother asked sternly.

"Yes mummy I am not lying and I will never lie to you again" Amar said solemnly.

Amanpreet softened a bit on hearing this and pulled him closer. She wiped his tears and gently ruffled his hair.

She let him go with a very strong advice. "Lies can get you in deep trouble and you stand to lose a great deal by telling lies. So my dear son, be brave and always speak the truth" she said.

Amar made a funny face and hugged his mother tightly. They started laughing.

The incident of the mysterious shoeprint and Amar's witty answer was not disclosed to anyone else, even though Amanpreet had a very hard time getting his shirt clean again!

THE INTERVIEW

Sanjeev was waiting for his friend and group-mate Rakesh to return to the barracks. They had been out since early morning for the Group task.

He was at the Selection Centre East, Allahabad (now called Prayagraj) for the SSB (Services Selection Board) test. It was the penultimate day of the SSB test and the second day of Group task which forms a part of the entire SSB test.

Suddenly he heard a JCO outside call out, "Chest number 24! Your interview will be today at 2 PM." He went on to call out the chest numbers of other candidates who were to appear for the interview that afternoon. Sanjeev noted that his friend Rakesh's chest number 26 had also been called out.

The Interview is a very crucial stage of the SSB test and Sanjeev wanted to be sure about the time of his interview. He went to check the list of interviewees for the day on the notice board outside the office of the Interviewing officer (IO). He saw that he was to be the first candidate to be interviewed in the afternoon of that day and the time was 2 PM sharp (immediately after lunch). He also checked for the time of Rakesh's interview and saw that it was slated for 3 PM.

He walked back to the barracks and met Rakesh on the way. He too, was going to check the list for the time of his interview. They stopped to greet each other.

"Rakesh, your interview is at 3 PM and mine is at 2 PM" Sanjeev informed him.

"Does that leave us time for the outing we had planned for, in advance?" Rakesh asked.

"I hope so, but we must not get distracted by our plans for the evening. The interview is very vital for our selection to the NDA. We must, both of us, do well and be among the selected candidates" Sanjeev stated confidently.

"Yes, I understand what you mean and we shall try to do well" Rakesh answered.

The two friends walked back to the barracks and lay down on their cots which were adjacent and tried to catch some much needed rest after a gruelling day of Group task. They tried to recall all that they had discussed among themselves in preparation for the SSB interview.

The SSB interview is the most 'dreaded' stage of the SSB test where every candidate has to come face to face with the Interviewing officer who is a high ranking officer of the armed forces. In order to avoid intimidating the candidates with his rank, the IO is not in uniform but in plain clothes during the interview.

The interview generally lasts for about half an hour and each candidate is required to report to the IO's office at least five minutes before the scheduled time.

"Let's get ready and go for lunch" said Sanjeev, somewhat refreshed by the little rest. Rakesh had been thinking deeply about the interview but his thoughts were cut short by Sanjeev's words.

Both of them got up and dressed in appropriate clothes (plain trousers and matching shirt) and went to the mess. They were among the first to arrive for lunch and were served immediately. On finishing their lunch, Sanjeev checked his watch for the time; it was 1:45 PM.

He took leave of Rakesh.

"Do well! Wish you all the best!" Rakesh wished him and firmly shook hands with him.

"Thank you! I hope to do well. See you soon" Sanjeev said and went towards the IO's office.

Rakesh went back to the barracks to wait, before leaving for his interview.

On reaching the IO's office, Sanjeev realized that he was ten minutes early. He settled down in a chair and waited to be summoned. He was asked to enter the IO's room at exactly 2 PM.

He went in and turned to face the IO and wished him smartly. The IO's office was neat and tidy. There were very few things around and the IO sat behind a big table in civilian clothes. He was a middle- aged man and looked very healthy. The IO asked Sanjeev to sit in a chair opposite him.

The interview commenced with Sanjeev's introduction and the IO asked him a wide variety of questions ranging from history, current affairs and general knowledge. Sanjeev felt that the most tricky questions were the ones on 'situation reaction' which were cleverly designed to unravel the candidate's personality, integrity and values.

The interview lasted a little over half an hour. Sanjeev was quite drained when the interview got over and he was finally asked to leave. He walked back to the barracks and Rakesh was waiting for him there.

Rakesh jumped up from his cot on seeing Sanjeev. He rushed to meet his friend and thumped him on the shoulder. "How did it go?" he asked.

Sanjeev took some time to reply. "I think I have done well" he said, a little unsure of himself.

"Good! Good! Now it is my turn. Wait for me here and be cheerful" said Rakesh as he hurriedly left for his interview.

"Best of luck" Sanjeev shouted after him.

Sanjeev really wanted Rakesh to succeed. On getting to know Rakesh, Sanjeev had liked him very much. They had become close friends in a matter of a few days. So much so that Sanjeev considered him to be a better and deserving candidate than himself.

He picked up a book to read as he waited for Rakesh to return after his interview. His mind was not in reading, for the day's events had been exhilarating and tiring at the same time. The excitement and thrill had been simply, too much for him.

At length when Rakesh returned, Sanjeev looked at him questioningly and immediately put aside his book. Rakesh saw the look of curiosity in his eyes and burst out laughing.

"What's so funny?" asked Sanjeev.

"Nothing" said Rakesh. "It's just that I had a little adventure during the course of my interaction with the IO" he explained.

"Tell me about it" Sanjeev asked, getting even more curious.

"You won't believe that I got to interview the IO at the end of my interview. He was completely bamboozled by what I said" Rakesh said, continuing to giggle.

"Will you tell me about it, now!" said Sanjeev, getting impatient.

Rakesh told him of the experience of that afternoon.

At the end of the interview, the IO had asked him, "Gentleman! I have asked you many questions; would you like to ask me any questions?" Rakesh had been very surprised at the openness of the IO.

He narrated the whole experience to his friend in a lively manner and in complete detail as it had occurred that afternoon. “Sanjeev, this is how it transpired, down to the last detail” said Rakesh as he began to speak:

“Sir, may I know your name?” Rakesh asked hesitantly.

“I am not at liberty to tell you that” the IO said in a deep voice.

‘Sir, may I know your rank? Rakesh asked him immediately.

“I am a Commander” the IO informed Rakesh.

Rakesh had paused briefly and let the fact soak in.

At the very next moment he said, “You are from the Navy, Sir!”

“Yes, of course” the IO nodded.

“But Sir, there’s a Commander in the Air Force also” Rakesh said doubtfully.

“What! A Commander in the Air Force! What are you saying, gentleman!” the IO exclaimed.

Rakesh tried to look calm and replied, “But Sir! That is a Wing Commander.”

The IO looked relieved at the correction and remarked “Yes, that’s right.”

Thereafter, Rakesh had been asked to leave and the interview was over.

Sanjeev sat mesmerized on hearing about Rakesh’s audacity during the brief interaction with the IO.

"Dear friend you were very bold in doing this. I hope it doesn't backfire and have a negative impact on your result" Sanjeev said thoughtfully.

"I don't think so, but it doesn't bother me. In any case I enjoyed my interview" said Rakesh jovially.

He pulled Sanjeev up by his elbow and said confidently "Don't worry too much; we are both going to the NDA. Now let's go to the Civil Lines market and enjoy ourselves."

Sanjeev smiled at him as they walked out towards the gate to hail a rickshaw to take them to the market.

The next day was the 'Final Conference' and thereafter the results were declared. The chest numbers 24 and 26 were called out again among those of the successful candidates.

Rakesh pulled Sanjeev aside as they filed out of the room.

"The IO must have had a keen sense of humour so as not to be annoyed at my questions yesterday" Rakesh said with a wink.

"Yes! Your witty answer was a bit too much for him, though" said Sanjeev smiling broadly.

Both the friends hugged each other tightly and burst out laughing.

www.ingramcontent.com/pod-product-compliance
Lightning Source LLC
La Vergne TN
LVHW041118150826
845673LV00007B/2107

* 9 7 9 8 8 9 2 3 3 3 3 7 5 *